A Note to Parents

Welcome to REAL KIDS READERS, a series of phonics-based books for children who are beginning to read. In the classroom, educators use phonics to teach children how to sound out unfamiliar words, providing a firm foundation for reading skills. At home, you can use REAL KIDS READERS to reinforce and build on that foundation, because the books follow the same basic phonic guidelines that children learn in school.

Of course the best way to help your child become a good reader is to make the experience fun—and REAL KIDS READERS do that, too. With their realistic story lines and lively characters, the books engage children's imaginations. With their clean design and sparkling photographs, they provide picture clues that help new readers decipher the text. The combination is sure to entertain young children and make them truly want to read.

REAL KIDS READERS have been developed at three distinct levels to make it easy for children to read at their own pace.

- LEVEL 1 is for children who are just beginning to read.
- LEVEL 2 is for children who can read with help.
- LEVEL 3 is for children who can read on their own.

A controlled vocabulary provides the framework at each level. Repetition, rhyme, and humor help increase word skills. Because children can understand the words and follow the stories, they quickly develop confidence. They go back to each book again and again, increasing their proficiency and sense of accomplishment, until they're ready to move on to the next level. The result is a rich and rewarding experience that will help them develop a lifelong love of reading.

For Alex and Rootie-Toots
—D. E.

Special thanks to Sara's Prints for providing pajamas
and to Oreck for providing the vacuum cleaner.

Produced by DWAI / Seventeenth Street Productions, Inc.
Reading Specialist: Virginia Grant Clammer

Library of Congress Cataloging-in-Publication Data
Eaton, Deborah.
   Monster Songs / Deborah Eaton; photographs by Dorothy Handelman.
       p.   cm. — (Real kids readers. Level 2)
   Summary: A little boy comes to his big brother for help in getting rid of the monster
under his bed.
   ISBN 0-7613-2054-7 (lib. bdg.). — ISBN 0-7613-2079-2 (pbk.)
   [1. Monsters—Fiction. 2. Brothers—Fiction. 3. Fear—Fiction.]
I. Handelman, Dorothy, ill. II. Title. III. Series.
PZ7.E1338Mk 1999
[E]—dc21   98-34283
                                                                                          CIP
                                                                                          AC

pbk: 10 9 8 7 6 5 4 3 2 1
lib: 10 9 8 7 6 5 4 3 2

Monster Songs

By Deborah Eaton
Photographs by Dorothy Handelman

M
The Millbrook Press
Brookfield, Connecticut

"Jack," said Hal. "Jack, wake up!"
He pulled down the sheet on his
brother's bed.

Jack pulled the sheet back up.
"Go away, Hal," he said.
"It is late. Go back to sleep."

"I can't," said Hal.
"There is a *monster* in my room."

Jack groaned.
"There is a monster in my room too,"
he said. "And his name is Hal!
Why don't you go get Mom?"

"Because I want you," said Hal.

Jack groaned again.
But he got up and went to Hal's room.

7

"Okay. Where is the monster?"
said Jack.

"Under my bed," said Hal.
"He is big and bad.
I could hear him singing.
He sings monster songs."

"What is a monster song?" asked Jack.
"What does it sound like?"

"Like this," said Hal.
"*OOoooOOooo!*"

"Stop it!" said Jack.
"That was the wind you heard.
That was not a monster."

9

"It was too," said Hal.
"I can show you what he looks like."
He drew the monster for Jack.

"Yuck!" said Jack. "He is an ugly one."

Hal's eyes filled with tears.
"Make him go away," he said.

"All right. Don't cry!" said Jack.
"I will get rid of him for you.
Just let me think."

Jack was a good thinker.
He walked around and around.
He rubbed his chin.

"I know!" he said.
"Give me a red marker, Hal."

"What do you think?" said Jack.
"We can put it on your door."

14

"Okay," said Hal.
"But what if my monster can't read?
He doesn't look very smart."

"You are right," said Jack.
He began to think again.
He walked around and around.
He rubbed his chin.
He made a thinking face.
"I know!" he said.
"We will scare him away."

Jack sat down by the bed.
"*BOO!*" he yelled.

"*Eeeek!*" yelled Hal.

"Sorry," said Jack.
"I didn't mean to scare you.
I will think again."

He walked around and around.
He rubbed his chin.
He made a thinking face.
He even hung upside down.
"I know!" Jack said.
Then he ran to get
something.

"What about this?" he said.
"It will suck the monster right up."

Hal shook his head.
"That thing is too loud," he said.
"It would wake up Mom and Dad.
Besides, the monster is too big."

"You know what, Hal?" said Jack.
"There is really no such thing
as a monster."

"I guess you are right," said Hal.
"I made this one up in my head.
First he was small.
Then he got bigger and bigger."

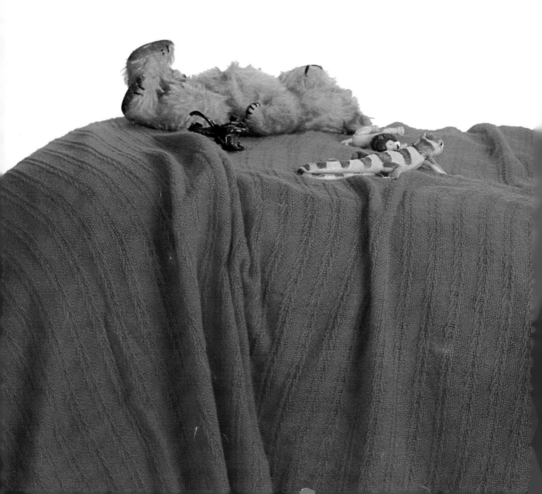

"You can get rid of him," said Jack.
"I know you can, Hal."

Now it was Hal's turn to think.
He walked around and around.
He rubbed his chin.
He made a thinking face.
He even hung upside down.

"I know!" he said.
"I will think him small again.
Then you can catch him."

"Good," said Jack.
"I will catch him in this box.
Think hard, Hal.
Make him small . . .
smaller . . .
smaller . . .
I got him!"

"Good work, Hal," said Jack.
"No more monster songs!
No more monsters under your bed.
Now you can go back to sleep."

"Okay," said Hal. "I will try.
But what about the ghost
in my closet?"

Phonic Guidelines

Use the following guidelines to help your child read the words in *Monster Songs*.

Short Vowels

When two consonants surround a vowel, the sound of the vowel is usually short. This means you pronounce *a* as in apple, *e* as in egg, *i* as in igloo, *o* as in octopus, and *u* as in umbrella. Short-vowel words in this story include: *bad, bed, big, box, but, can, Dad, get, got, Hal, him, his, let, Mom, not, put, ran, red, rid.*

Short-Vowel Words with Consonant Blends

When two or more different consonants are side by side, they usually blend to make a combined sound. In this story, short-vowel words with consonant blends include: *bent, hung, just, singing, sings, songs, stop, suck, went, wind, yuck.*

Double Consonants

When two identical consonants appear side by side, one of them is silent. In this story, double-consonants appear in the short-vowel words *filled, rubbed, will, yelled,* and in the all-family, the words *all* and *small.*

R-Controlled Vowels

When a vowel is followed by the letter *r*, its sound is changed by the *r*. In this story, words with r-controlled vowels include: *first, for, hard, marker, more, scare, smart, turn, work.*

Long Vowel and Silent E

If a word has a vowel and ends with an *e*, usually the vowel is long and the *e* is silent. Long vowels are pronounced the same way as their alphabet names. In this story, words with a long vowel and silent *e* include: *face, late, like, made, make, name, wake.*

Double Vowels

When two vowels are side by side, usually the first vowel is long and the second vowel is silent. Double-vowel words in this story include: *groaned, read, sheet, sleep.*

Diphthongs

Sometimes when two vowels (or a vowel and a consonant) are side by side, they combine to make a diphthong—a sound that is different from long or short vowel sounds. Diphthongs are: *au/aw, ew, oi/oy, ou/ow.* In this story, words with diphthongs include: *down, drew, loud, now.*

Consonant Digraphs

Sometimes when two different consonants are side by side, they make a digraph that represents a single new sound. Consonant digraphs are: *ch, sh, th, wh.* In this story, words with digraphs include: *catch, chin, such, that, then, there, think, thinking, this, what, where, why, with.*

Silent Consonants

Sometimes when two different consonants appear side by side, one of them is silent. In this story, words with silent consonants include: *back, ghost, Jack, walked.*

Sight Words

Sight words are those words that a reader must learn to recognize immediately—by sight—instead of by sounding them out. They occur with high frequency in easy texts. Sight words not included in the above categories are: *a, again, an, and, are, around, because, by, could, does, go, good, he, I, in, is, it, looks, me, my, no, okay, on, one, said, the, to, too, under, up, want, was, would, you, your.*